MW00709651

The First Christmas at the Rosebrier

Written and Illustrated
by
Beverly Rose

The Overmountain Press
JOHNSON CITY, TENNESSEE

ISBN 1-57072-149-1

Copyright © 2000 by Beverly Rose
All Rights Reserved
Printed in the United States of America

1 2 3 4 5 6 7 8 9 0

Dedicated to
Jesus Christ

Merry Christmas 2009
Josie!

May God's Blessings always
be upon you!

Love,
Linda, Greg & Boone

Montgomery and Mable Mole snuggled under the nice warm quilts Mable had made for their home. They could hear the cold winds blowing outside. It was hibernating time for the moles.

Suddenly, there was a strange noise like someone hammering at the front door. Then the sound of beautiful music wafted its way to Montgomery's and Mable's ears. Montgomery had to get up. He put on his bedroom slippers and went to the door.

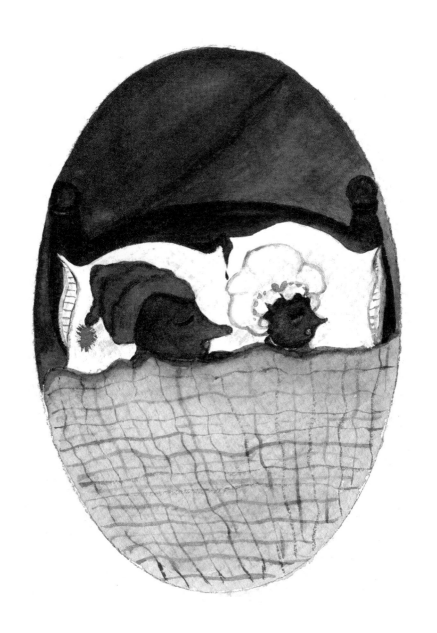

The snow was piled high around the door, and Montgomery had to push hard to open it. He opened the door and saw a beautiful wreath with a bright red ribbon and little carolers singing in front of his home. Montgomery did not understand, because he wasn't accustomed to being awake during the winter. He waved at the carolers and shut the door. He was shivering when he got back into bed. Snuggling under the quilts, a feeling of curiosity started in his stomach. He just had to find out what was going on!

He awakened Mable and told her he was going to see Mr. Rabbit. Montgomery dressed very warmly because it was bitterly cold. He slowly trudged through the thick snow. Some of the huge drifts were over his head!

Mr. Rabbit's door displayed a festive wreath just like the one at Montgomery's. He wondered what this meant. He knocked on the door, and Mr. Rabbit opened it with a smile on his face. He said, "Montgomery, what brings you out on a cold night like this?" Montgomery told him about the hammering, the singing, and the wreath.

In the next breath Montgomery asked, "What is going on?" Mr. Rabbit had a puzzled look on his face. "Well. . . it's almost Christmas," he said. Montgomery asked, "What is Christmas?" Mr. Rabbit could not believe his long ears! He thought everyone knew about Christmas. He asked "Have you really never heard about Christmas?" Montgomery answered, "No, Mr. Rabbit. I hibernate in the winter." Mr. Rabbit was relieved as he replied, "Montgomery, take off your hat and coat, we have a lot to talk about."

Mr. Rabbit told Montgomery that he first heard about Christmas from the owner of this farm and a little black headed girl. It was many years ago in late Autumn. He was looking for some fresh greens to nibble when he heard some voices. The farmer was standing beside a beautiful cedar tree pruning a few of the limbs. A tiny little girl with long black curls asked why he was cutting the pretty tree. The farmer said it was to be his Christmas tree. The little girl asked him, "What is Christmas?" The farmer answered, "Beverly you know what Christmas is." The little girl said, "But Uncle Royall I want you to tell me the story." The farmer sat down on an old tree stump, and the little girl climbed into his lap.

He began, "Christmas is an important birthday celebration. God's son, Jesus, was born on Christmas. People all over the world celebrate on this day." The little girl asked him, "Why do we give gifts on Christmas day?" The farmer replied, "It has been told that three kings traveled many miles with gifts to pay tribute to the Christ child. The tradition of giving gifts began a long time ago with these men."

"Who is Santa Claus?" asked the little girl. "Santa was a real live person," the farmer answered. "He was originally called Saint Nicholas. He was a Bishop of Myra in Asia Minor during the third century. Saint Nicholas was a kind and generous man, and he gave many gifts to people in need. The name Santa Claus was started in the United States. Many years ago people were not allowed to celebrate because they forgot the true meaning of the season."

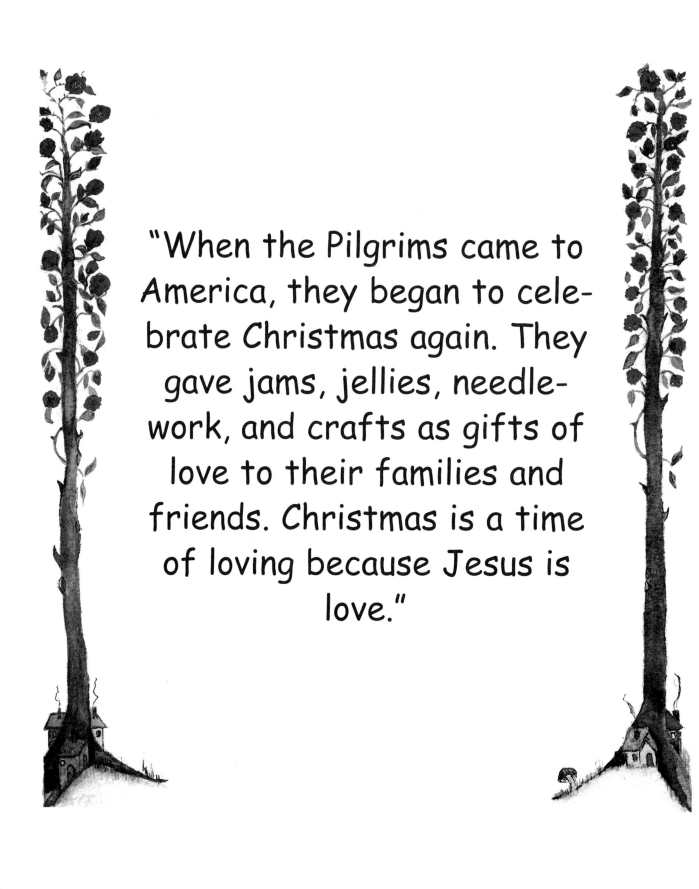

"When the Pilgrims came to America, they began to celebrate Christmas again. They gave jams, jellies, needlework, and crafts as gifts of love to their families and friends. Christmas is a time of loving because Jesus is love."

The little girl asked, "Why do we have Christmas trees?" The farmer said, "In ancient Rome--even before Christ--greenery was used symbol of good luck and purity. Therefore the tree is a symbol of the purity of the Christ child. When people are happy they love to celebrate and decorate at Christmas."

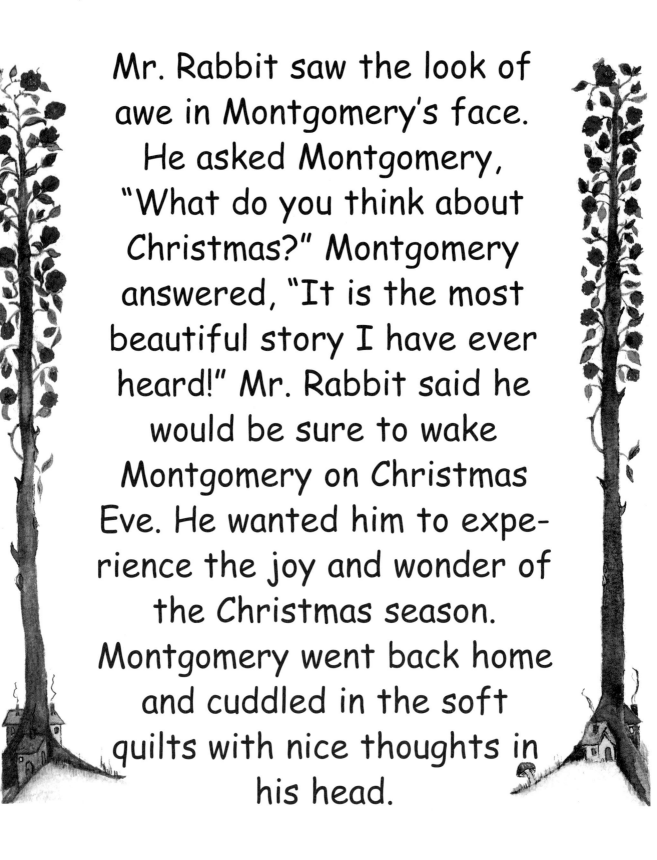

Mr. Rabbit saw the look of awe in Montgomery's face. He asked Montgomery, "What do you think about Christmas?" Montgomery answered, "It is the most beautiful story I have ever heard!" Mr. Rabbit said he would be sure to wake Montgomery on Christmas Eve. He wanted him to experience the joy and wonder of the Christmas season. Montgomery went back home and cuddled in the soft quilts with nice thoughts in his head.

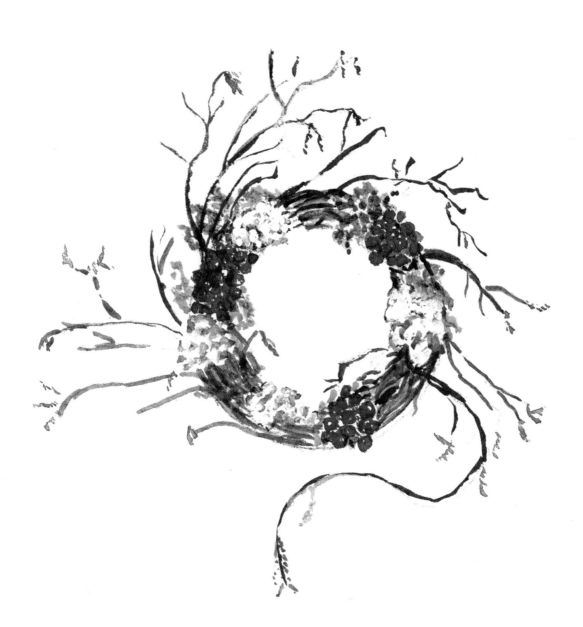

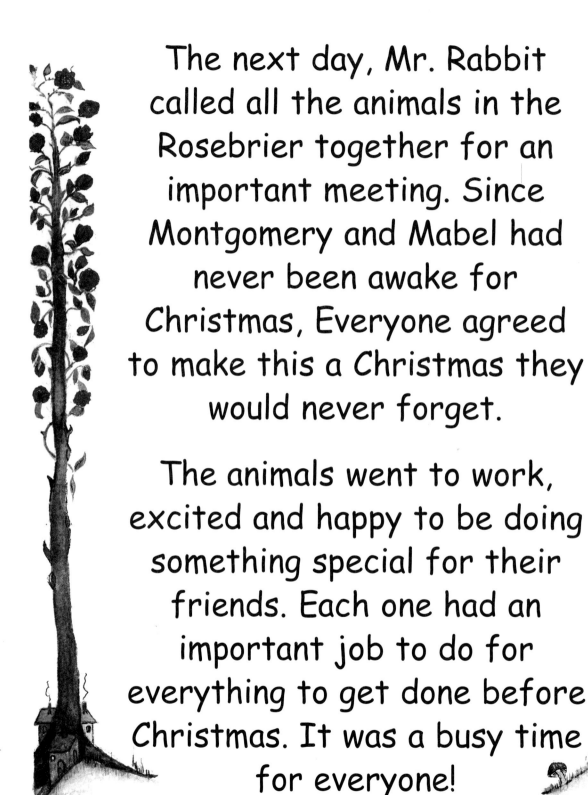

The next day, Mr. Rabbit called all the animals in the Rosebrier together for an important meeting. Since Montgomery and Mabel had never been awake for Christmas, Everyone agreed to make this a Christmas they would never forget.

The animals went to work, excited and happy to be doing something special for their friends. Each one had an important job to do for everything to get done before Christmas. It was a busy time for everyone!

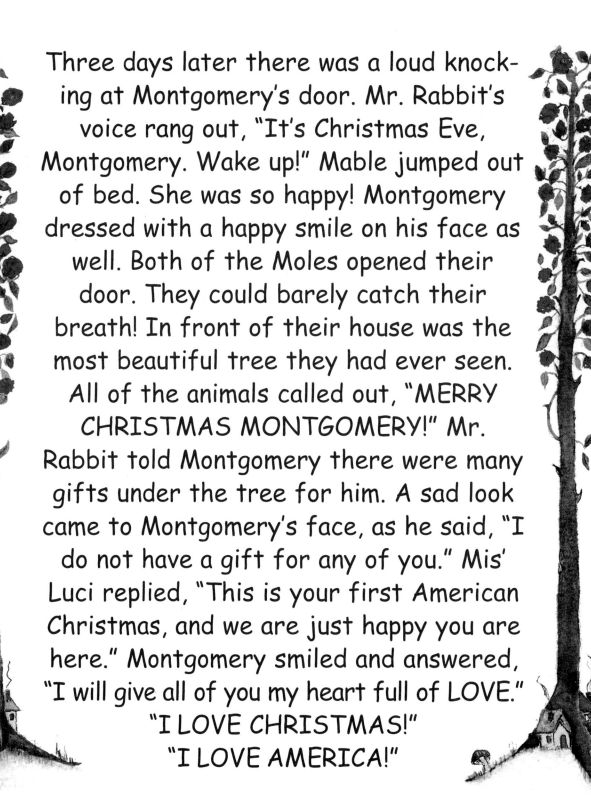

Three days later there was a loud knocking at Montgomery's door. Mr. Rabbit's voice rang out, "It's Christmas Eve, Montgomery. Wake up!" Mable jumped out of bed. She was so happy! Montgomery dressed with a happy smile on his face as well. Both of the Moles opened their door. They could barely catch their breath! In front of their house was the most beautiful tree they had ever seen. All of the animals called out, "MERRY CHRISTMAS MONTGOMERY!" Mr. Rabbit told Montgomery there were many gifts under the tree for him. A sad look came to Montgomery's face, as he said, "I do not have a gift for any of you." Mis' Luci replied, "This is your first American Christmas, and we are just happy you are here." Montgomery smiled and answered, "I will give all of you my heart full of LOVE."
"I LOVE CHRISTMAS!"
"I LOVE AMERICA!"

O Come All Ye Faithful

O come all ye faithful, joyful and triumphant,
O come ye, O come ye to Bethlehem;
Come and behold Him born the King of angels;

O come , let us adore Him, O come, let us adore Him,
O come, let us adore Him, Christ, the Lord.

Sing, choirs of angels, sing in exhultation,
O sing, all ye bright hosts of heaven above;
Glory to God, all glory in the highest;

O come , let us adore Him, O come, let us adore Him,
O come, let us adore Him, Christ, the Lord.

Yea, Lord, we greet Thee, born this happy morning,
Jesus, to Thee be all glory given;
Word of the Father, now in flesh appearing;

O come , let us adore Him, O come, let us adore Him,
O come, let us adore Him, Christ, the Lord. Amen.